My First Story

Birmingham & Warwickshire

Edited by Jenni Bannister

About this book ...

First published in Great Britain in 2012 by:

 Young**Writers**

Remus House
Coltsfoot Drive
Peterborough
PE2 9BF
Telephone: 01733 890066
Website: www.youngwriters.co.uk
All Rights Reserved
Book Design by Ali Smith
© Copyright Contributors 2012
SB ISBN 978-0-85739-949-6

Welcome!

Young Writers was established in 1991 with the aim of encouraging writing skills in young people and giving them the opportunity to see their work in print. As a part of this imprint, My First Story was designed for Key Stage 1 children as an introduction to creative writing and to promote an enjoyment of reading and writing from an early age.

The simple, fun storyboards give even the youngest and least confident writers the chance to become interested in literacy by giving them a framework within which to shape their ideas. As well as this it also allows older children to let their creativity flow as much as possible, encouraging the use of imagination and descriptive language.

We believe that seeing their work in print will inspire a love of reading and writing and give these young writers the confidence to develop their skills in the future.

Our defining aim at Young Writers is to foster the talent of the next generation. We are proud to present the resulting collection of regional anthologies, containing the first stories from our authors of the future.

CONTENTS

Goodyers End Primary School, Bedworth

Highters Heath JMI School, Kings Heath

Hurley Primary School, Atherstone

Lickey Hills Primary School, Rednal

Moor Green Primary School, Moseley

Oakfield Primary School, Rugby

St Anthony's RC School, Kingshurst

Timberley Primary School, Shard End

Ward End Primary School, Ward End

Woodloes Primary School, Warwick

Wyken Croft Primary School, Coventry

Imagine ...

**Each child was given the beginning
of a story and then chose one of five
storyboards, using the pictures and their
imagination to complete the tale.**

The Beginning ...

One night Ellie was woken by a tapping at her window.

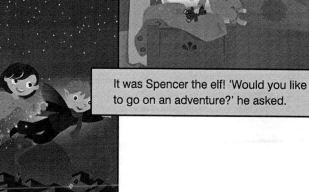

It was Spencer the elf! 'Would you like to go on an adventure?' he asked.

They flew above the rooftops. Soon they had arrived ...

MAGICAL ADVENTURE

Storyboard 1

JUNGLE TALE

Storyboard 2

PIRATE ADVENTURE

Storyboard 3

SPACE STORY

Storyboard 4

Zoo Adventure

Storyboard 5

The
Stories

Beaconside Primary
& Nursery School
Rubery

Isabelle's Zoo Adventure

At the zoo they were excited to be there, so they walked in.

Then they had a ride on an elephant's back through the zoo.

Soon they met a panda called Lucy. Ellie hugged Lucy.

Then the elephant took them somewhere and he took them to …

A monkey! He was eating a banana. So Ellie ate one too.

Finally, Ellie said goodbye to the elephant and she went home.

Isabelle Topalli (7)
Beaconside Primary & Nursery School, Rubery

Kian's Pirate Adventure

Once there was a girl and a boy and they were sailing across the water.

Suddenly, they stopped on an island and they found some treasure. Ellie was standing on it.

Later, a pirate came with a sword and the teddy was hiding behind Spencer.

Next, the pirate made Spencer walk the plank and he put one leg up and he was by the flag.

Next, Spencer and Ellie jumped in the water and two dolphins jumped up and they rode on them.

In the end, Spencer and Ellie and Teddy walked home and they were worn out.

Kian Ross (7)

Beaconside Primary & Nursery School, Rubery

Toby's Magical Adventure

Once there was a pink and white unicorn in magic land.

Suddenly, they saw a big, fierce dragon. Ellie's teddy hid behind her legs.

They ran away from the big, fierce dragon. They were very scared.

Suddenly, they found a pretty unicorn. They climbed on the unicorn.

On the way they saw a witch. The witch gave teddy a lollipop.

They had a ride on the witch's magic broomstick.

Toby Richard Bailey (6)
Beaconside Primary & Nursery School, Rubery

Louie's Pirate Adventure

At night Spencer and Ellie went on a boat. They ended up on an island.

They found some treasure, some gold and silver treasure. Suddenly, a pirate came. He said, 'That's my treasure.'

Then Ellie said, 'No, that's my treasure.'
The pirate said, 'OK, I will lock you up and you will walk the plank.'

Spencer jumped off the plank, then Ellie jumped off the plank.

They landed on a dolphin. The pirate said, 'Come here.'
Ellie said, 'No, I won't.'

They walked home and Spencer said goodbye.

Louie Field (7)
Beaconside Primary & Nursery School, Rubery

Emily's Magical Adventure

At a magical world there was a unicorn. It was sad. Ellie said, 'What's the matter?' So they stroked it and climbed on it.

Then they saw a dragon on the way. It was red and it had a pointy ear.

They ran away. It was breathing fire.

They were happy again.

Then they saw a witch.

She let Ellie and Spencer go on the magic broomstick.

Emily Burns (7)
Beaconside Primary & Nursery School, Rubery

5

Kulab's Magical Adventure

Soon they arrived at a fairytale land. They met a rainbow unicorn. She had a magic horn.

They saw a big, terrifying dragon. He was breathing fire.

The dragon chased Ellie and Spencer and Mr Teddy too.

The unicorn came running and she saved them. She used her magic to put them on her back.

A good witch came. She said 'Hello, I know what you need, a broom!'

So they got the broom and went home.
'Do not go without me,' said Teddy.

Kulab Angliner Foster (6)
Beaconside Primary & Nursery School, Rubery

Joshua's Zoo Adventure

They arrived at the zoo. First they saw an elephant. They had a ride on him.

Next, they went to interesting trees. The elephant gave them a ride.

They saw a polar bear. It was amazing. She had a baby. It was a miracle and amazing.

They walked and walked. At last they arrived.

They saw a chimpanzee. He was funny and he was brown. He was eating a banana.

Then Spencer had to go home. 'Bye-bye,' he shouted.

Joshua Dunne (6)
Beaconside Primary & Nursery School, Rubery

Roan's Pirate Adventure

One night Ellie was woken by a tapping at her window. It was Spencer. They flew over the homes.

They found an island. It had treasure, it had gold treasure boxes and they saw a boat and it had a pirate on it.

He said to Ellie and Spencer, 'Hello, don't get that treasure.'

'You walk the plank.'

Dolphins rescued Ellie and Spencer and Ellie was tired, so the dolphins took them to an old home.

They saw a home. 'Look, a home. Let's go to the home.'

Roan Smith (6)
Beaconside Primary & Nursery School, Rubery

Shauna's Magical Adventure

At a magical land they met a pink unicorn. The unicorn had wings.

Suddenly, they spotted a red dragon. He was called Jack. Jack was very scary.

The dragon blew fire. Ellie and Spencer ran as fast as they could.

Ellie and Spencer spotted the unicorn. They both jumped onto the unicorn. She was pretty.

When they got off the unicorn, they met a mean witch.

Ellie and Spencer flew off into the sky on the witch's broom.

Shauna Sherwood (7)
Beaconside Primary & Nursery School, Rubery

Joshua's Pirate Adventure

When they got there, they saw an island. Spencer rowed the boat while Ellie sat down.

Suddenly, they reached the island and found some treasure. Then Spencer saw a pirate ship.

Out came a pirate captain and unleashed his sword. He made Spencer walk the plank.

When Spencer walked the plank, Ellie looked scared and so did Teddy because they thought he would drown.

Spencer walked the plank and flew and grabbed Ellie, then jumped on a dolphin.

They grabbed the captain's hat and took Ellie home.

Joshua Addis (6)
Beaconside Primary & Nursery School, Rubery

James's Pirate Adventure

They had arrived at a sunny island. Soon they had some lunch.

When they got there they had some spades and they dug up treasure.

Ellie and Spencer suddenly saw a pirate come.

They hopped on the boat, but the captain made Spencer walk the plank.

When they got in the sea, the whales came and they rode home.

Suddenly, they came back home. Ellie and Spencer got home.

James Morton (6)
Beaconside Primary & Nursery School, Rubery

Emily's Zoo Adventure

They soon arrived at the zoo and rode on the elephant. Ellie's teddy was on the trunk.

The elephant was hungry. Spencer looked after Ellie. Soon they got off.

They saw a panda. It was black and white. It was cute.

Soon they got back on the elephant and it dropped them at the monkey's side.

They had a banana. Ellie had a banana. Spencer did not.

They headed back to Ellie's house and dropped her home.

Emily Rose White (6)
Beaconside Primary & Nursery School, Rubery

Shani's Pirate Adventure

When they had landed, they saw a boat in the river. They took a ride.

They sailed until they saw an island. They got to a island. They saw a treasure.

Then they saw a pirate. He talked really loudly. He scared the life out of them.

The pirate was nice and he let them come on his boat in the sea.

Then they rode on two dolphins. They were cute and blue and white.

They had a pirate hat and when they got home they had a cup of juice.

Shani Forbes (6)
Beaconside Primary & Nursery School, Rubery

Mia's Magical Adventure

One night Ellie was woken by a tapping at her window. Ellie's bedroom looked sparkly.

Suddenly, a dragon came. The dragon had big pointy teeth and claws.

Ellie was scared and Spencer the elf was scared of the dragon.

Then they met a unicorn to ride to the lollipop tree.

Then when they got there, a witch came out of a lollipop tree.

But they made it home.

Mia Tisdell (6)
Beaconside Primary & Nursery School, Rubery

Lydia's Magical Adventure

Once there was a little girl and a boy and they saw a pink and purple unicorn.

Suddenly, they saw a dragon. It was fierce and it was green. It had a yellow tummy.

After, they had to run away from the dragon and it blew fire out.

They found the unicorn and they climbed on her.

Suddenly, they saw a witch. She pointed at them.

They hopped on the witch's broom and went home.

Lydia Bessent (6)
Beaconside Primary & Nursery School, Rubery

15

Kyle's Space Story

When they got there Ellie was so surprised.

Finally, they landed on a planet. They saw an alien.

When they weren't looking, a ship came on top of them with an alien in it.

Zoom! Ellie came up so quickly. The alien was friendly. He showed Ellie in space.

No! There was a bad alien on a planet.
'No fear, Bob is here!' Bob threw an arrow at it.

Then they went back home.

Kyle Barnsley (6)
Beaconside Primary & Nursery School, Rubery

Phoebe's Pirate Adventure

When they landed, they were in a boat. Ellie was so amazed.

Spencer rowed the boat to an island. At the island they found treasure. Ellie jumped on the treasure box.

When Spencer and Ellie were about to open the box, they met a big, jolly pirate.

The pirate was so kind he let them a ride on his pirate ship. Spencer walked the plank.

Ellie and Spencer had a ride on dolphins. It was really fun!

Later on, they swam to shore and walked home. It was great being a pirate!

Phoebe Gates (6)
Beaconside Primary & Nursery School, Rubery

Micah's Jungle Tale

At the jungle they swung on vines. Teddy said it was fun so they swung faster and faster. They said they loved it.

They stopped at something swirly. It had a tongue. It was yellow and orange. It was a snake.

They ran really fast and they didn't see it again.

Then on the way back they saw a lion. The lion looked at them. They were scared.

The lion wanted Ellie, Spencer and Teddy to hop aboard. They went on then it moved.

Then they all swung home really fast on the vines. Then they went to bed.

Micah Blackwood (6)

Beaconside Primary & Nursery School, Rubery

Binley Woods
Primary School
Coventry

Corbin's Pirate Adventure

Ellie and the elf sailed in a boat.

They found a treasure chest.

A pirate arrived.

They put the treasure back on the ship.

They sailed back home on the dolphins.

They arrived home.

Corbin Turner (6)

Binley Woods Primary School, Coventry

Jessie's Magical Adventure

At the magical world of Lollipop Land, they arrived on a pony called Silver. She was very kind and caring and she was made out of candy.

When Ellie and Spencer were walking, they came across a mean dragon called Fiery Fred. He was always breathing fire at people. 'See, I told you he was mean!'

Fiery Fred liked eating children after he had cooked them with his fiery breath! So he chased Ellie and Spencer.

The children ran and ran until they found Silver. They were really, really happy! Then Ellie started to cry. 'I want to go home,' she sobbed.

So Silver told the children to go and see Wonder the witch because she could help them. Wonder let them borrow her broom to get home.

Then Ellie and Spencer set off and they arrived at home in Candy Land. Ellie jumped for joy to be at her lovely home.

Jessie Troup (7)
Binley Woods Primary School, Coventry

21

Sam's Space Story

They flew higher and higher.

When they landed on the moon, they could see the stars.

Then an alien picked them up in his ship.

They flew with the alien.

Then they saw a monster.

Spencer and the alien took Ellie home.

Sam Hewett (6)
Binley Woods Primary School, Coventry

Wilf's Pirate Adventure

In a tropical lemonade sea, they saw a sweet island.

Ellie found a chest full of chocolate coins. 'Yummy,' Ellie said.

'Argh! Stop eating my coins!' shouted Captain Rotten Teeth.

The captain made them walk the plank!

Two marshmallow dolphins came to the rescue.

Ellie and Spencer got home with all their teeth!

Wilf Sansum (7)
Binley Woods Primary School, Coventry

Dani's Pirate Adventure

One day a little boy and girl were sailing their boat.

They met a pirate. The pirate said, 'Don't steal my treasure!'

Soon, they found a crown for their teddy bear. It was small.

The girl and the boy got on a ship and the boy fell in the water.

The dolphins caught both of them.

Because they had a great adventure, they both went home.

Dani Parmar-Diggle (6)
Binley Woods Primary School, Coventry

Jaymee's Magical Adventure

They heard something behind them and they held on tight to the unicorn.

They thought it was safe and jumped off the unicorn, but suddenly a dragon appeared.

As they ran away, the dragon blew fire out of his mouth at them.

The unicorn came to get them and took them to a magical witch.

The witch said they could have one wish. They wished to go home.

Their wish came true and they lived happily ever after.

Jaymee Pouncett (6)
Binley Woods Primary School, Coventry

Jamie's Pirate Adventure

They rowed their boat and found a desert island.

There was a big wave and a treasure chest washed up on the sand.

A pirate suddenly appeared, waving his cutlass at them.

Captain Hook made Spencer walk the plank.

Two dolphins came to their rescue and the children held on tight to the fins …

All the way home.

Jamie Talbot (6)
Binley Woods Primary School, Coventry

Kelcy's Magical Adventure

Ellie and the elf were riding on a unicorn in the woods.

They met a big, scary dragon that blew flames out of his mouth.

Ellie and the elf were very scared and ran away.

The unicorn saved them.

Ellie and the elf went to see a witch.

The elf used the witch's broom to take Ellie home.

Kelcy Wilson (6)
Binley Woods Primary School, Coventry

27

Ava's Magical Adventure

They landed in Lollipop Land on a beautiful unicorn called Rainbow.

The unicorn went. They saw a dragon that could breathe fire.

They ran back towards the hill where they could see Rainbow waiting for them.

When they got back, Rainbow had blue spots all over her. Ellie rubbed at the spots.

And ... Rainbow turned into a witch! Before she could cast a spell on them ...

Ellie and Spencer grabbed her broom and flew home. What an adventure!

Ava McKenzie (6)

Binley Woods Primary School, Coventry

Thomas' Magical Adventure

They had arrived at a magical land. Then they got on a unicorn.

But then a big dragon came and scared Ellie. The dragon breathed fire at Ellie and Spencer.

They ran as fast as they could and got on the unicorn.

They were galloping along, smiling away and giggling as the wind was blowing.

But then a scary witch with a wart on her cheek scared Spencer.

But they escaped and flew home while it was still dark. They both smiled a happy smile.

Thomas Good (6)

Binley Woods Primary School, Coventry

Ruby's Space Story

Once there was a girl called Ellie. She had a friend, he was an elf and he was called Spencer.

Suddenly, they saw an alien and he saw them too.

The alien went into his spaceship and sucked Ellie up.

Next, Ellie was in the alien's spaceship.

Next, they saw a monster and he stuck his tongue out.

Next, Ellie went home and went to bed.

Ruby Grace Barnacle (6)
Binley Woods Primary School, Coventry

Lucy's Magical Adventure

The unicorn flew into the forest. She was scared of the trees.

The dragon saw Ellie and Spencer. They were frightened.
'Go,' said Spencer.
'No,' said Ellie.

'Run!' said Ellie.
'Run!' said Spencer.
'I am scared of a fire,' said Ellie.

The unicorn landed on the ground.

Next the witch came. She was scary. Spencer said that it is rude to point.

They flew home to have a sleep. Their mummy said, 'Where have you been?'

Lucy Parker (6)
Binley Woods Primary School, Coventry

Izzy's Magical Adventure

One day Ellie and Spencer went to a magical world.

Suddenly, a dragon went at them. They ran away, the dragon ran.

The dragon was too slow and couldn't catch them because they went too fast.

Soon, a unicorn saw them.

There was a witch. 'You must go,' she said.
So they went.

They flew home and Ellie was sleepy.

Isabelle Greaves (5)

Binley Woods Primary School, Coventry

Katie's Space Story

Once there was a boy called Spencer and a girl called Ellie. They went to the moon.

They went to the edge of the moon and picked stars from the sky.

An alien was spying on Ellie. Next, the alien zapped Ellie in the alien ship.

After that the alien took Ellie for a ride in his spaceship.

Then they saw a scary monster with his mouth open and he stuck his tongue out.

Then alien took Ellie and Spencer home to bed and they went to sleep.

Katie Macaffer (5)
Binley Woods Primary School, Coventry

Bishops Itchington
Primary School
Southam

Isabel's Jungle Tale

In the hot, steamy, green jungle me and Elfie swung through the jungle vines. It felt like I was flying.

Suddenly, a great big, slimy, hungry snake slithered up to me and Elfie and he looked very hungry.

The slimy snake slide up and said , 'Yum!' in the most mysterious voice. I ran away from it.

Then I saw a lion. He jogged up and said, 'Hello, what are you doing here? Hop on my back.'

We all hopped on his back and ran off.

When I had a ride home, I recognised it was still the gloomy night and we said goodbye.

Isabel McFerran (6)
Bishops Itchington Primary School, Southam

Paige's Jungle Tale

In the leafy, wet, hot, steamy jungle, Spencer the elf and Ellie were swinging.

Then a fat, slimy, slithery snake sprang out of the trees, planning to eat them.

'Run!' cried Spencer.
Ellie and Spencer ran for their lives, desperate to get away from the snake.

Suddenly, a lion roared out and said in a ginormous voice, 'Jump on my back.'

They ran through the whooshy trees. *Whoosh! Whoosh!* Swing. *Wheee.*

Finally, it was time to go home. Spencer and Ellie swung home for dinner.

Paige Wheeler (6)
Bishops Itchington Primary School, Southam

Amelia's Jungle Tale

In a hot, magnificent jungle, they arrived on a green leafy vine.

Suddenly, a big, scary snake appeared out of some leaves.

He managed to scare Ellie and Spencer.

Then out of the leaves sprung a big, cute, lovely lion.

He let Ellie and Spencer the elf ride on his big, furry back.

Suddenly, green, leafy vines swung along and took them back to the dark, black night.

Amelia Blumberger (6)
Bishops Itchington Primary School, Southam

Emily's Jungle Tale

In a hot, steamy jungle swinging on long vines.

They met a slithery snake who wanted to eat them!

They were terrified so they ran away.

Next, a cuddly lion came and pounced on a leaf.

He kindly gave them a ride back home.

Finally, it was a starry night when they got back.

Emily Maughan (5)
Bishops Itchington Primary School, Southam

Seth's Jungle Tale

In the hot, gleaming jungle, Ellie and Spencer were very busy.

Until they saw a slimy, wiggling snake and it looked hungry!

They dashed away in fear.

Until they met a furry, yellow lion.

They rode on it and found out it was nice.

They found some vines and swung home. They went to sleep.

Seth Harper (7)
Bishops Itchington Primary School, Southam

Bishopton Primary School
Stratford-upon-Avon

Rhys' Zoo Adventure

Ellie and Spencer flew to the beautiful zoo.

They crept on the large elephant.

Ellie and Teddy cuddled the large panda bear.

They rode on the big, grey elephant.

Ellie ate a yellow banana while Teddy swung on the vine.

Ellie and Teddy got back home on the grey elephant.

Rhys Bryant (6)
Bishopton Primary School, Stratford-upon-Avon

Josie's Zoo Adventure

Ellie and Spencer the elf went to the zoo.

They met a grey elephant.

Then they met a giant panda. Spencer the elf held the baby giant panda.

Soon they were on the grey elephant's back.

They met a funny monkey. Ellie and the monkey ate bananas while Teddy was swinging on a vine.

Finally, Ellie arrived back home to her comfy bed.

Josie Hancox (6)
Bishopton Primary School, Stratford-upon-Avon

Ben's Zoo Adventure

At that moment, Spencer the elf took Ellie to a zoo and they saw a zebra.

Ellie had a ride on a hairy elephant and on their way they saw some other animals.

Ellie had a hug from a panda. She liked the panda.

Ellie had another ride on the elephant. The elephant was soft.

Next, Ellie ate a banana with a monkey and the monkey was soft and cosy.

After that she had a ride on an elephant again, but Ellie enjoyed her adventure.

Ben Carey (6)
Bishopton Primary School, Stratford-upon-Avon

Zofia's Jungle Tale

Ellie and Spencer the elf swung on a tree, just like the swings.

Suddenly, they met a snake. They were petrified. Next, the snake said to them, 'I am hungry! I want to eat meat!'

Then Ellie and Spencer ran like a cheetah because they were scared.

At the third place, Spencer and Ellie met a nice friendly lion.

They had lots of fun because they had a ride on his back.

Finally, they swung back to Ellie's warm house.

Zofia Kubacka (6)
Bishopton Primary School, Stratford-upon-Avon

Dominik's Jungle Tale

They swung in the tree.

They saw a bad snake. He nearly caught them.

Spencer and Ellie ran at the bad snake. It was very scared.

Then they saw a good lion.

They rode on the lion's back.

Then they arrived home.

Dominik Fiodorow (6)
Bishopton Primary School, Stratford-upon-Avon

Jedrzej's Jungle Tale

They swung on the tree.

They saw a snake. The snake hissed at Spencer and Ellie.

They ran away from the slithery snake.

Then they saw a lion.

They had a ride on the lion.

Then they swung back home.

Jedrzej Jakielski (7)
Bishopton Primary School, Stratford-upon-Avon

Coleshill CE
Primary School
Coleshill

Faith's Magical Adventure

One day Amy and Louie sat on the magic unicorn.
'Let's go on an adventure,' said Louie and they fluttered away.

They saw something an orangey-purply red colour. Amy said, 'Come on.' But when they got there, it was …

A dragon! It was howling and breathing fire. Barnaby, Amy's bear, Amy and Louie ran as fast as they could.

The children climbed onto the pretty unicorn. 'Let's go on an adventure.'
Soon they were galloping at full speed.

Soon they came to a land of lollipops. Barnaby licked a red, sweet lollipop. All of a sudden, a witch appeared.

The children ran as fast as they could, climbed onto the witch's broomstick and went whizzing home.

Faith Jennings (6)
Coleshill CE Primary School, Coleshill

Milly's Magical Adventure

One day Sam and his sister, Amy, were playing in the garden when a unicorn appeared from nowhere.

Rosie the unicorn took Sam and Amy on a magical adventure. A dragon scared Rosie and she ran off.

Sam and Amy ran away from the dragon to find Rosie.

Sam and Amy found Rosie, they jumped on Rosie's back and she ran off very fast.

They saw an old witch but she was pretending to be nice.

The witch gave them the broomstick and then they flew back home.

Milly Young-Turner (6)
Coleshill CE Primary School, Coleshill

Madison's Magical Adventure

When they got there they found a little pony named Lilly. They decided to go on it.

Lilly got hungry, so Ellie and Spencer looked for apples. But on the way they met a dragon.

So Ellie and Spencer ran away from the scariest dragon in the whole world.

Eventually they found Lilly, so Lilly took them to a safe place.

Then they met a nasty old witch. 'Come with me, children,' she said. So they stole the broom.

They both got on the broom, then Spencer took Ellie home.

Madison Alsop (6)
Coleshill CE Primary School, Coleshill

Tobias' Jungle Tale

At the jungle they were having fun swinging in the creepy jungle.

After swinging, they saw right in front of them was a snake slithering around.

While Spencer and Ellie ran, the snake said, 'I want you to be my lovely, delicious dinner tonight.'

When they met the lion, the lion was staring at them. Spencer and Ellie were worried.

When they made friends, the lion let Ellie and Spencer go on its back.

At last they got home and swung back.

Tobias Wakefield (7)

Coleshill CE Primary School, Coleshill

Lee's Pirate Adventure

One morning Spencer and Ellie went out in their boat.

They found an island with a treasure chest filled with gold coins.

At the island they met a bad pirate and he wanted the chest for himself.

He made Spencer walk the plank. Ellie was scared that she was next.

Spencer and Ellie were saved by two dolphins.

They started to walk home holding hands.

Lee Cuthbert (6)

Coleshill CE Primary School, Coleshill

Reiss' Jungle Tale

They went to a jungle. They were swinging on vines.

They saw a snake.

The snake scared them and they ran away.

They found a lion. It was a friendly lion.

The lion gave them a ride on his back.

Then they swung home on a vine.

Reiss Price (6)
Coleshill CE Primary School, Coleshill

Zara's Zoo Adventure

At the zoo Ellie and Spencer could see monkeys, elephants and panda bears. They couldn't believe that they were at the zoo.

They rode on an elephant and the teddy bear sat on the trunk.

The elephant took them to cuddle the panda.

Then the elephant took them to see a monkey.

When they arrived to see the monkey, he gave Ellie a banana and little bear had a swing in the tree.

Soon, the adventure had ended. It was time for Ellie to go home and take Spencer back to Elf land.

Zara McCorry (6)
Coleshill CE Primary School, Coleshill

Luci's Zoo Adventure

They arrived at the front entrance of the zoo where a sneaky elephant was peeping from behind the fence.

They rode on the grey elephant with Ellie's special teddy on its trunk into the zoo. They saw trees, leaves and branches.

Soon they said goodbye to the big elephant and set off deeper and darker into the zoo. When they got tired they found a panda bear.

After that they found the grey elephant and rode on him again. They went on more into the zoo.

They soon met some silly monkeys who were eating bananas. Teddy was swinging on the green vines.

At last it was time to go. Ellie left the teddy with the elephant and set off home.

Luci Cave (6)
Coleshill CE Primary School, Coleshill

Renée's Jungle Tale

There once were two children who got lost in the jungle. They swung on the vines to keep safe and well.

Suddenly, one of them fell. They landed by Sammy, a long, slimy snake. That's when they realised they had made a mistake.

Then they met Brian, a big lion who had a lampshade on his head.

He was happy to give them a ride with their friend, Ted.

The girl and boy soon thought home would bring the most joy and swung through the trees to get home for dinner.

Renée Hadley (6)
Coleshill CE Primary School, Coleshill

Ava's Pirate Adventure

Then they went on a boat and rowed to the island.

They found some treasure. Spencer saw a ship.

They spoke to the pirate and he said, 'You kids, that's my treasure to find.'

'Oi, you come here,' said the pirate.
Quickly, they escaped and jumped in the water.

Luckily, they got away on dolphins.
'Oi, come back, kids.'

Finally, they got home and lived happily ever after.

Ava Edmeade (7)
Coleshill CE Primary School, Coleshill

Bradley's Magical Adventure

Riding on a horse through the park in the hot sunshine.

They bumped into a dragon who scared them.

They ran as fast as they could.

They lost the dragon and were safe.

They met an old, skinny witch who tried to snatch their lollies.

They'd had a long day and now it was time to go to bed.

Bradley Steers (7)
Coleshill CE Primary School, Coleshill

60

Goodyers End
Primary School
Bedworth

Seren's Jungle Tale

One day Jenny, Tom and their teddy, Tim, went to play in the jungle. They swung on vines.

While they were there they met a mighty snake that wanted to eat them up.

Jenny, Tom and Tim ran deeper into the dark, scary jungle.

They ran into a huge, fearsome lion. They were petrified because they thought he would eat them.

But he was friendly and he wanted to take them for a ride through the jungle.

They wanted to go home and swung through another set of vines and went home.

Seren Kalay (6)
Goodyers End Primary School, Bedworth

Rahana's Pirate Adventure

One day there lived a girl and a boy. The beautiful girl was called Rahana and the boy was called Michael. They were brother and sister.

The next day they went to the beach in a boat. They played pirates. Rahana was the captain and Michael was the pirate.

Suddenly, a really scary pirate appeared. Rahana and Michael were petrified. He was pretending that he was friendly.

The pirate said, 'Walk the plank.'

Suddenly, Rainbow and Rain, the dolphins, got Rahana and Michael.

Then they walked home and lived happily ever after.

Rahana Duffy (6)
Goodyers End Primary School, Bedworth

Casey-Leigh's Magical Adventure

One day two children rode a magical unicorn to the woods.

A dragon came and frightened them.

The children ran to the other side of the woods.

The unicorn rescued them and took them to see a witch.

The witch cast a spell on them to send them home.

They arrived home at midnight and told their mum about their adventure.

Casey-Leigh Jones (6)
Goodyers End Primary School, Bedworth

Sophie's Magical Adventure

Once there was a golden unicorn who was friends with two shy, frightened kids.

The children were terrified of the fierce dragon who breathed fire.

No matter how fast the children ran, they could not escape from the scary dragon.

The speedy unicorn flew to the children's rescue. They climbed on their hero's back.

The unicorn took the children to a friendly witch. They thanked the unicorn for the help.

The kind witch gave the lost children her broomstick which flew them back home.

Sophie Claybrook (6)
Goodyers End Primary School, Bedworth

Katie's Zoo Adventure

Alice and Peter are going to the zoo.

Alice and Peter are riding on the elephant.

Alice and Peter are cuddling the panda.

Alice and Peter are going through the jungle.

Alice is eating a banana with the gorilla.

Alice is going home and Peter is going back to the jungle.

Katie Johnson (6)
Goodyers End Primary School, Bedworth

Declan's Pirate Adventure

Sam and Ann went on a boat ride.

They found some golden treasure.

Along came a pirate who stopped them getting the treasure.

He took them onto his pirate ship and made them walk the plank.

They got away on a dolphin.

They went home dressed as pirates.

Declan Jay (5)
Goodyers End Primary School, Bedworth

Reece's Jungle Tale

Jack and Sarah were swinging on the tree.

They saw a hissing snake.

They had to run to a safe place.

They found a nice, friendly lion.

The lion said, 'Do you want to have a ride on my back?'

So the lion took them home.

Reece Hinton (5)
Goodyers End Primary School, Bedworth

Libby's Jungle Tale

Jack and Jill were out in the jungle having fun with their friend, Ted.

When they saw a snake, they thought it was friendly until it began to hiss at them.

Then they ran away because they thought it was going to eat them.

Then they saw a tiger. The tiger smiled at them. They smiled back.

He growled to ask if they would like to go for a ride. They said yes.

He took them to where they lived and they carried on playing till teatime.

Libby Costello (5)
Goodyers End Primary School, Bedworth

Roxanne's Pirate Adventure

Harry and Mia went to Treasure Tree Island.

They saw treasure in a big, shiny box.

Pegleg pirate took the coins and the children.

'Walk the plank!' he said. He was angry.

They got a ride from two kind dolphins.

They never went to Treasure Tree Island again.

Roxanne Carol Biggs (5)
Goodyers End Primary School, Bedworth

William's Space Story

Emily and William were floating in space.

They were catching stars.

Ellie and Teddy were caught.

But they had fun.

They saw an alien.

They went back.

William Duquid (5)
Goodyers End Primary School, Bedworth

Emily's Pirate Adventure

The children were sailing to an island.

They found a treasure chest full of gold and a teddy wearing a crown.

The children met a pirate.

They sailed onto a pirate ship.

They swam with dolphins.

Then they went home.

Emily Louise Duguid (6)
Goodyers End Primary School, Bedworth

Keaton-Lee's Zoo Adventure

Rosie and Josh went to the zoo.

They saw an elephant and they went on top of him.

They saw a panda and they played with the baby panda.

They rode on the elephant some more.

Rosie met a monkey and had a banana tea with him.

Then the elephant gave Josh and Rosie a ride back home.

Keaton-Lee Northall (6)
Goodyers End Primary School, Bedworth

James' Pirate Adventure

Having a nice time on the water in a boat looking for treasure.

They found the treasure.

They saw a pirate on the island.

They went on a pirate ship.

They swam with dolphins.

They had a good day. Time to go home.

James Moore (7)
Goodyers End Primary School, Bedworth

James' Space Story

Lucy and James left Earth with Lucy's bear called Bloobs. They went to Mars.

James was picking some stars. There was an alien called Girfee. He was looking at James.

Lucy was beginning to lift into the alien's ship. She looked petrified.

She had a great time with the ship and the alien.

A big, sloppy monster was trying to attack the alien's ship.

They went home. The boy had to stay behind.

James Clark (6)
Goodyers End Primary School, Bedworth

Logan's Zoo Adventure

Milly and Billy went to the zoo. Milly took her teddy called Pogo.

At the zoo, Milly and Billy went on an elephant. Pogo sat on the elephant's trunk.

Then Milly and Billy went to see the pandas. Milly and Pogo cuddled the panda.

Milly and Billy and Pogo went on a ride on the elephant.

Milly and the gorilla had a banana. Pogo swung on the trees.

Billy took Milly and Pogo home and waved goodbye.

Logan Constable (7)
Goodyers End Primary School, Bedworth

Paige's Zoo Adventure

The children went to the zoo and they saw an elephant.

They got on the elephant and they saw the bear.

Then they saw some polar bears.

They went on the elephant again.

They saw monkeys and Holly ate a banana.

Their friend went home and they lived happily ever after.

Paige Smith (6)
Goodyers End Primary School, Bedworth

Leah's Magical Adventure

Connor and Caitlin were having a magnificent time on their unicorn.

Suddenly, they heard a huge flapping noise.

It was a dragon and it started to chase them.

They ran and ran until they had reached their unicorn.

Then they saw a wicked witch but instead, she was nice.

The witch helped Connor and Caitlin get home on her broomstick.

Leah Wilks (7)
Goodyers End Primary School, Bedworth

Joshua's Magical Adventure

Reece had a dream that he went on a unicorn with Annie.

They found a dragon who was very scary and he breathed fire on them.

They ran away as fast as they could.

They got back on their unicorn and started to go home.

They were almost home when they met a kind witch.

She let Reece and Annie ride her broomstick all the way home.

Joshua Jay (5)
Goodyers End Primary School, Bedworth#

79

Grace's Pirate Adventure

Jake and Lizzie went searching for treasure.

They found lots of treasure on Coconut Island.

'Argh! That's my treasure!' said the pirate.

The pirate took the children onto his ship and made them walk the plank.

The dolphins rescued them and saved the day.

Jake and Lizzie made it home in time for tea.

Grace Whinmill (5)
Goodyers End Primary School, Bedworth

Sam's Space Story

Sam and Lillie flew through space with Mr Tiddles.

Sam and Lillie landed on the moon. Sam found a star.

Lillie and Tiddles got sucked up by the ship.

Lillie flew in a ship with an alien.

Sam and Lillie saw a monster.

The alien dropped Sam and Lillie back home.

Sam Harriman (6)
Goodyers End Primary School, Bedworth

Olivia's Space Story

There was a little girl and boy who flew up into the stars.

The girl and boy were collecting the stars when an alien appeared.

A light sucked the girl and her teddy into a spaceship.

The little girl made friends with the alien and they flew in the spaceship.

Suddenly, the alien tried to get them with his big, long tongue, but they escaped.

Then the alien and the boy took the girl home and they said goodbye.

Olivia Suett (5)
Goodyers End Primary School, Bedworth

Rosie's Space Story

Once upon a time there was a boy and a girl who jumped off Earth to see some aliens.

Aliens and children have never met. 'What shall I do?'

The children went into the spaceship.

They went flying all over space with other aliens.

The alien sucked up a monster. He was horrible so they dropped him.

The alien took the girl home and the boy back to space.

Rosie Hutchinson (5)
Goodyers End Primary School, Bedworth

Highters Heath
JMI School
Kings Heath

Joshua's Jungle Tale

First we swung from trees.

Then we saw a snake.

We ran away.

Next we met a lion.

So we went on the lion's back.

Finally we went home on a rope.

Joshua Heath
Highters Heath JMI School, Kings Heath

Gracie's Magical Adventure

First, they are riding a unicorn.

Next, a dragon was scaring them.

Then, they were running away from the dragon.

Then, they hopped onto a unicorn.

Next, they visit the witch.

Lastly, they flew home.

Gracie Lardener
Highters Heath JMI School, Kings Heath

Qismet's Magical Adventure

First they went on a unicorn.

Next they saw a dragon.

Then they ran away.

Then they went on the unicorn.

Then they saw a witch.

Then they went home.

Qismet Zaman (6)
Highters Heath JMI School, Kings Heath

Leah's Magical Adventure

First they rode a unicorn.

Next they got scared.

Then they ran.

They rode the unicorn.

Next they met a witch.

Then they rode home.

Leah Shepherd (5)
Highters Heath JMI School, Kings Heath

Ellie's Pirate Adventure

First they were in a boat.

Next, there was treasure.

Next, they met a pirate.

They went on a pirate ship.

Next, they were riding on a dolphin.

Next, they were going home.

Ellie Heath
Highters Heath JMI School, Kings Heath

Frankie's Zoo Adventure

They are going to the zoo.

They are on an elephant.

Next, they are meeting a panda.

Next, they are on an elephant.

Next, they met a chimpanzee.

Next, the little girl went home.

Frankie Sandland-Baksh
Highters Heath JMI School, Kings Heath

Neive's Magical Adventure

First they went on a unicorn.

Then they were scared.

Then they ran.

Then they were on the unicorn again.

They were scared.

Then they flew back home.

Neive Clarke-Turvey
Highters Heath JMI School, Kings Heath

Kyle's Magical Adventure

First there was a unicorn.

The dragon was scary.

So they ran away.

Next they rode on the unicorn.

They saw a nasty witch.

Finally, they went home.

Kyle Allen
Highters Heath JMI School, Kings Heath

Hurley Primary School
Atherstone

Will's Magical Adventure

Molly and Tom went on their unicorn.

Molly and Tom were scared.

So they ran away with their teddy.

Molly and Tom got back on the unicorn.

Molly and Tom met a witch.

They flew home on her broomstick.

Will Freeman (5)
Hurley Primary School, Atherstone

Adam's Magical Adventure

They landed and got on a unicorn. He was called Bite.

He went to show them a dragon called Fierce. He was scary.

Spencer and Ellie ran away saying, 'Argh! It could bite us!'

Spencer and Ellie got back on Bite to ride to a witch.

She was a nice witch and she gave Ellie's teddy bear a lollipop.

She let them get on her broomstick to ride back to Ellie's house.

Adam Hurley (5)
Hurley Primary School, Atherstone

Leah's Magical Adventure

In a magical place called Pony Land, they took a ride on a magnificent unicorn.

They met a scary dragon who was breathing fire.

Ellie, Spencer and Teddy ran away as fast as they could.

They jumped back on Celestia the unicorn and carried on their adventure.

They met a friendly witch in a red cape.

She lent them her broomstick to take them home to Ellie's mummy and daddy.

Leah Marshall (6)
Hurley Primary School, Atherstone

Luke's Magical Adventure

They met a magic unicorn.

They saw a scary dragon.

They ran away from the dragon.

They got back on the unicorn.

They met a nice witch.

They went home on her broomstick.

Luke Connolly (6)
Hurley Primary School, Atherstone

Sydney's Magical Adventure

At Unicorn Land they met the queen unicorn.

They went on a little ride. The dragon came to fire them. He breathed flames.

The children ran and ran. They were feeling very frightened.

The queen unicorn rescued them and flew away.

They met a candy witch, then they ran and ran.

They borrowed the witch's broom and the flew home together.

Sydney Stokes (5)
Hurley Primary School, Atherstone

Joshua's Magical Adventure

Ellie and Spencer went on the unicorn in Elf Land.

The mean dragon blew red and yellow fire at them.

Ellie and Spencer ran away from the dragon. They were scared.

They got away from the dragon on the magic white unicorn.

Next, they met a good witch. She gave them her broomstick.

Spencer took Ellie home by the light of the moon!

Joshua Ouston (5)
Hurley Primary School, Atherstone

Ryan's Magical Adventure

Teddy, Ellie and Spencer went for a ride on a unicorn.

Then they met a dragon.

'Let's run!' said Ellie.

They went back to the unicorn.

Next, they saw a witch.

She gave them a magical broomstick.

Ryan Smith (5)
Hurley Primary School, Atherstone

Tara's Space Story

...and Spencer arrived on the moon after a wonderful flight through
...e.

...he moon they met Mercury the alien and helped her collect stars to
...er spaceship.

...star power worked so they all went for a space ride.

...le flying, they saw Mercury's cousin, Neptune. He was having a
...ce battle.

...h Ellie's help they defeated the space monster by twisting him up in
...own tongue!

...me for home.' Ellie waved goodbye to her new friends and snuggled
...ck into bed.

...ra Clark (7)
...ckey Hills Primary School, Rednal

Faith's Magical Adventure

They are going to Australia. They are having fun.

A dragon tried to scare the unicorn away. The children are scared.

They are running because the dinosaur is trying to chase them.

The unicorn is coming to save them.
'Thank you. Thank you so much.'

'There's a witch! Help, help, please.'
'Somebody, please!'

They are getting on a broom. They like brooms.

Faith Wilson (6)
Hurley Primary School, Atherstone

Charlie's Magical Adventure

At a unicorn forest, they met Daisy.

They saw a dragon.

The children ran and ran away.

Daisy's mum saw a teddy and the children.

They came to a nasty witch. She scared them.

They took her broomstick and flew home.

Charlie Bentick (5)
Hurley Primary School, Atherstone

Lickey Hills Primary School
Rednal

Ellie
spac

On t
fix h

The

Whi
spa

Wit
his

'Ti
ba

T
Li

104

William's Pirate Adventure

Ellie and Spencer are rowing on the still waters of the Octopus Sea searching for adventure.

They find the treasure and Ellie stands on top of the treasure box.

The fierce pirate, whose name was Eyepatch, didn't let them have the precious, golden treasure. 'It's mine,' he said.

Eyepatch is so angry, steam comes out of his ears. He makes them walk the plank!
'Help!' cried Ellie.

They got onto the blue dolphins. The dolphins went up, down, up, down on the water.

When the dolphins had taken them to the shore, they walked home and they said, 'Thank you.'

William Hobbs (6)

Lickey Hills Primary School, Rednal

Joshua's Space Story

They flew into space. The Earth looked small.

They arrived at the planet. There was an alien.

The alien took Ellie and her teddy.

They made friends. They flew in the spaceship.

An alien attacked the ship.

Spencer and the alien took Ellie home.

Joshua Coles (6)
Lickey Hills Primary School, Rednal

Marielle's Jungle Tale

They found themselves in a jungle. Ellie and Spencer swung on vines. Ellie said, 'This is fun!'

When they got down, they saw a snake. They both screamed very, very loudly.

They ran and the snake smiled and laughed. The snake hissed when they escaped.

They saw a lion. He said, 'Hello, can I be your friend?'
'Yes,' said Ellie.

They rode on his back. 'This is great fun!' said Ellie.

They hopped off the lion's back. They could see home so they said goodbye to the friendly lion.

Marielle Sime (6)
Lickey Hills Primary School, Rednal

Ruby's Magical Adventure

Ellie and Spencer found a unicorn. Spencer asked the unicorn if they could ride on her. The unicorn saw a big dragon. She ran off as fast as her legs could carry her, leaving the children behind.

Rooarrrr! said the dragon, breathing fire from his mouth.
'Argh!' said Ellie.
The dragon said, 'Do you want to have a feast in my house?'
'No!' said Spencer.

As fast as their legs could carry them, they ran away from the dragon screaming.
'Come on,' said Ellie to Teddy.
'OK.'

Then they found the unicorn again.
'I'm so glad we found you. We thought that we would never find you,' said Ellie.

Just then they met a witch.
'Hello there, my dears. Are you lost?'
'No! We are just going for a walk.'
'OK! If you need me, just call me.'
'OK.'

But they didn't have any problems. Once they got a little bit tired, Spencer said, 'It's time to go home.'
'OK,' said Ellie and off they went.
When they arrived, Ellie fell asleep.

Ruby Mills (6)
Lickey Hills Primary School, Rednal

110

Jenni's Zoo Adventure

They went to the zoo to see some animals.

Ellie and Spencer went on a strong elephant.

They went to hug the pandas because pandas have soft fur.

Next, Ellie and Spencer went back to the strong elephant for a ride.

The monkey gave Ellie a banana to eat.

Spencer took Ellie home on the strong elephant again.

Jenni Morgan-Lee (6)
Lickey Hills Primary School, Rednal

Olivia's Jungle Tale

Ellie and Spencer are swinging on lush green vines through the jungle.

They are talking to a snake not realising that he is really nasty.

The nasty snake is chasing Ellie and Spencer through the dangerous jungle.

They meet a friendly lion hiding behind some bushes.

The lion takes them home so they can go on another adventure.

They are swinging on the vines to get home to see her mummy.

Olivia Brown (7)
Lickey Hills Primary School, Rednal

Lauren's Zoo Adventure

Spencer the elf took Ellie to the gigantic zoo in China. Suddenly, they saw an enormous elephant.
'Hello, my name is Dimples,' bellowed the elephant.
'Wow, wow! I never thought an elephant could talk.'
'Would you like to come for a walk?'
'Yes please!'

Finally, they found the panda.
'Oh look, a cuddly panda!' said Ellie.
'Hello, my name's Cuddles. Do you like my baby?'
'Oh yes.'

'What is your favourite animal?'
'A monkey,' they said together as they clambered back onto the elephant's back.

'Oh hello, would you like a banana?' said the monkey. 'By the way, my name is Checo.'
'Yes I do want a banana, please.'

'Bye-bye, nice to see you,' said Ellie. 'Thank you Spencer, Dimples, Cuddles, Checo. Thank you everyone!'

Lauren Bethel (7)
Lickey Hills Primary School, Rednal

Thomas' Pirate Adventure

Spencer and Ellie row over to a deserted island.
'I hope there is some food,' said Ellie.

Ellie says, 'Where did all this treasure come from?'
'I think it belongs to those pirates,' said Spencer.

A grumpy old pirate shouted, 'Pass that back now!'
Ellie and Spencer were terrified.

'Get off that plank or I will chop off your head!' boomed the grumpy old
pirate.

Just as Spencer was about to fall in, two dolphins came dashing to
help.
'This is fabulous,' said Ellie.

Spencer took Ellie to a store to get pirate outfits.
'This will remind you of your adventure,' he said.

Thomas Pulford (6)
Lickey Hills Primary School, Rednal

Oliver's Jungle Tale

In the jungle swinging on the vines.

Then a scary snake popped up.

The children ran away frightened.

Then they came across a friendly lion.

The lion was going to take the children home.

Then they spotted the vines and swung home.

Oliver Turbill (7)
Lickey Hills Primary School, Rednal

Maximus' Jungle Tale

Ellie, Spencer and Teddy are swinging in the jungle having fun.

Suddenly, they see a big, nasty snake wrapped around a tree, about to eat them for tea.

Spencer and Ellie are scared of the snake, so they run as fast as their legs can run.

Then they met a very wise lion looking for some deer for lunch and one for tea.

The lion takes them out of the creepy jungle to Ellie's house.

Then they swing to Ellie's window under the glimmering moon.

Maximus Claydon (6)
Lickey Hills Primary School, Rednal

Maxted's Space Story

They flew for a long time.
'Can we go to space?' asked Ellie.
Spencer replied, 'Yes, of course we can.'

They reached for the stars! They both caught lots of stars but they didn't notice the alien behind them going, 'Mwa ha ha ha!'

The alien went to his spaceship and put it into open door mode.
'Come aboard both of you.'
And so they did.

The alien took Ellie and Spencer on a tour around space.
'Would you like to see my pal Tongue Flicker Licker?'
'Wow! Of course we would.'

They looked down and couldn't believe how long his tongue was. It reached for the stars and he waved with it.

The alien and Spencer delivered Ellie safely back home. They all said goodbye and hoped they would meet again soon.

Maxted Weekes (6)
Lickey Hills Primary School, Rednal

Thomas' Pirate Adventure

Ellie and Spencer were rowing in the sea because they were looking for an adventure.

Ellie and Spencer found treasure on an island. It was sparkly and shiny gold coins.

Oh no, a pirate found Ellie and Spencer. He wanted the treasure.

The bad pirates put Ellie and Spencer on their boat. They made Spencer walk the plank.

Ellie and Spencer found some dolphins in the sea. They let them ride them.

They helped them get back home safely. What a great adventure they'd had.

Thomas Powell (7)
Lickey Hills Primary School, Rednal

118

Laura's Zoo Adventure

Ellie and Spencer arrived at the zoo. There was a giraffe and an elephant.

They had an elephant ride with a baby panda.

They found a mummy panda. She cuddled Ellie and Spencer was holding her baby.

They got onto the elephant with the little baby panda tied up.

Ellie met a monkey called Dimples who gave Ellie a banana.

The sun went down and the moon came up. Spencer dropped Ellie off. She said goodbye.

Laura Sparkes (7)
Lickey Hills Primary School, Rednal

Ethan's Space Story

They flew above the rooftops. Soon they had arrived at space.

When they got to space they waved at Earth.

After that an alien ship saw them. Suddenly, the alien ship sucked them up.

Next, the alien took the girl home.

When the alien took the girl home, they got stuck because there was a gigantic alien in the way.

A while later the little girl got home.

Ethan Burke (6)
Lickey Hills Primary School, Rednal

Josh's Space Story

In space they saw a planet. It was Planet Murgen.

An alien spotted Ellie and Spencer on his planet.

The alien wanted to make friends so he beamed Ellie up into his spacecraft.

Then alien took Ellie on a trip around the stars.

Then they noticed a bad alien, so they destroyed it.

It was time for Ellie to go to bed, so the alien and Spencer took her home.

Josh Wrafter (6)
Lickey Hills Primary School, Rednal

Grace's Magical Adventure

Once upon a time there was a lady called Ellie and her friend was called Jack.

They were riding on a unicorn until a dragon came. The unicorn ran off.

They ran and ran and Teddy was nearly left behind. He managed to catch up.

They found their unicorn and they set off on an adventure.

They found a good witch. They were scared, but she gave them something special …

Her broomstick. What an adventure!

Grace McArthur (6)
Lickey Hills Primary School, Rednal

Grace's Magical Adventure

Ellie, Spencer and Ted had a magical ride on a pink unicorn.

A big, angry dragon came and said he was going to eat them.

Spencer shouted, 'Run as fast as you can!'

Unicorn knew a friendly witch who could help them run away.

The children were scared, but the witch had an idea.

She gave them her broomstick to ride all the way home.

Grace Govier (6)
Lickey Hills Primary School, Rednal

Katie's Zoo Adventure

At the zoo.
'How exciting,' said Ellie. 'I have never been to a zoo.'

'This is a special zoo because the animals talk,' said Spencer.

The elephant said his name was Zoozoo and took them to see the baby panda.

Zoozoo said, 'Let's have lunch with a monkey.'
'That sounds good, let's go!' Ellie said.

Callum the monkey had bananas, Ellie's favourite.
'Let's eat!' said Callum.

It was getting late, so Spencer and Zoozoo gave Ellie a ride home before morning time.

Katie Griffiths (6)
Lickey Hills Primary School, Rednal

Charlie's Pirate Adventure

A boy called Ben took a girl named Jemima to a desert island.

On the island they found a treasure chest full of gold.

A pirate came and snatched the treasure from Ben and Jemima.

The pirate took Ben and Jemima on board his ship. They had to walk the plank.

Two dolphins were in the sea. Ben and Jemima climbed on the dolphins.

They were home safe and sound just before midnight.

Charlie Muir (6)
Lickey Hills Primary School, Rednal

Elliot's Pirate Adventure

Ellie and the elf arrived at a treasure island. They could see a big palm tree.

On the beach they found a treasure chest full of money and jewellery.

Suddenly, a pirate came and said, 'What are you doing with my treasure?'

'Come to my boat and you will have to walk the plank.'

As Ellie and the elf fell into the water, two dolphins rescued them.

They took them back home where they were safe and glad to be back.

Elliot Proctor (6)
Lickey Hills Primary School, Rednal

Alice's Zoo Adventure

Ellie opened her eyes and found, as if by magic, she was at the zoo with Spencer.

A very large but friendly elephant called Dumbo greeted the friends at the door.

'I shall show you around. Come meet my friend, Poppy the panda bear,' exclaimed Dumbo.
Spencer held baby Pingo panda.

Next, Dumbo decided a visit to Molly the monkey would be exciting. He scooped Ellie and Spencer onto his back.

Molly was eating bananas, so she said to the children, 'Come on, have a healthy snack with me.'

Dumbo decided to take Ellie back to her snuggly bed. Spencer waved goodbye and vanished in the sky.

Alice Gray (7)
Lickey Hills Primary School, Rednal

127

Jessica's Zoo Adventure

At the zoo, they were very excited to see all the animals.

First they saw the elephants. The elephant's name was Edward and he offered them a ride.

Edward took them to see Polly the panda and her baby, Pippa.

Then Edward took them to see Gary the gorilla.

Ellie and Gary had a banana together.

Edward and Spencer took Ellie home. They had a great adventure together.

Jessica Hislop (6)
Lickey Hills Primary School, Rednal

Dylan's Pirate Adventure

In a boat and then we were rowing the boat.

We got onto an island and then I jumped on the chest.

Pirates saw us and the captain wanted the gold.

Then he made us walk the plank. I was worried and scared.

We fell onto dolphins and I thought I was lucky. It was fun.

Then he took me home. I was happy.

Dylan Kane (6)
Lickey Hills Primary School, Rednal

Orla's Magical Adventure

When they arrived they found a magical pony.

Then suddenly, they saw an enormous dragon.

They ran so fast. They caught the teddy and carried it. They ran out of breath and stopped.

'Look,' said Spencer, 'our pony is here.'
'Oh great, perfect, we love our pony.'

'Spencer, why is there a witch here?'
'I don't know. She looks horrible.'

'This is so good. We are going home. I'll miss you, Spencer.'
'I'll miss you, Ellie.'

Orla Holloway (6)
Lickey Hills Primary School, Rednal

Daniel's Jungle Tale

They went to the jungle and started to swing.

They saw a snake and it was very nasty to them.

So they ran away from the hissing snake.

Then a lion peeked out and said, 'Hello, my name is Leo.'

'Would you like to come with me?' he asked.

They saw their house in the distance. They shouted, 'Yippee! We are going home!'

Daniel Lyons (6)
Lickey Hills Primary School, Rednal

Callum's Jungle Tale

One day Jack, Lilly and Pudsey were playing in the jungle but …

They came across what they thought was a friendly snake but …

The snake turned out to be a scary, poisonous snake who wanted to keep Pudsey forever.

They bumped into Fred, the friendliest lion in the world. He said he would help them get away from the snake.

They jumped on Fred's back and he ran as fast as his strong legs would take him, safely away from the snake.

Thanks to Fred, he got them all safely home just in time for dinner.

Callum Hill (6)
Lickey Hills Primary School, Rednal

Lucy's Space Story

At space they flew in the air.

They landed on a planet and met an alien.

The alien took them into his spaceship.

They flew across the sparkly stars.

Then they met another scary alien.

Then they dropped Ellie home.

Lucy Arch (6)
Lickey Hills Primary School, Rednal

Jonah's Jungle Tale

Then they arrived at the jungle.

They walked and walked. Suddenly, a poisonous snake came to eat them up.

Then the children ran away.

Then they saw a lion. The lion was actually kind.

The lion took the children for a ride.

Then the children went home.

Jonah Loveridge (6)
Lickey Hills Primary School, Rednal

April's Magical Adventure

One evening Spencer said, 'Do you want to go on a magical adventure?'

Soon we were there. We met a terrifying dragon.

We were terrified by the dragon.

The unicorn saved us because she was king.

An ugly witch came. I was frightened.

We finally flew home.

April Parry (6)
Lickey Hills Primary School, Rednal

Luke's Magical Adventure

A unicorn was waiting to fly them high in the sky.

Next, a fierce dragon started to breathe fire at them.

Ellie and Spencer and little ted ran away as fast as they could.

The magic unicorn came to save them. The three climbed on his back and away they zoomed.

They then met a friendly witch and she gave little ted a lolly. It was getting late.

The nice witch gave them her broomstick to get home before the moon said goodnight.

Luke Bimson (7)
Lickey Hills Primary School, Rednal

Gypsy's Zoo Adventure

Ellie and Spencer arrived at the zoo. It was cold and dark. They were tired.

They met a magical elephant. Ellie knew he was magical because he was bright blue! He was called Mark.

He took them to see his friend Carole the panda and her baby, Jason.

Ellie and Spencer were tired and hungry, so Mark let them ride on his back to look for food.

They found a friendly gorilla called Dougie who gave them all bananas to eat.

It was getting late, so Mark and Spencer took Ellie home to her little house and bed.

Gypsy Jones (7)
Lickey Hills Primary School, Rednal

Emma's Magical Adventure

At a magical place they saw a beautiful unicorn with a sparkling mane.

Suddenly … a fire-breathing dragon woke up.
'Oh no!' said Ellie.

The dragon started to chase them, so they ran away.

The unicorn was waiting for them, so they got on and then galloped away.

At last they saw a kind witch. 'Do you want to use my broomstick?' she asked.
'Yes please,' said Ellie.
They climbed on and flew home.

Emma Clough (6)
Lickey Hills Primary School, Rednal

Daniel's Space Story

Ellie saw stars all around her. She said, 'Where are we?'
'Really,' said Spencer, 'we are in space.'

They saw a star and grabbed it.
'It is beautiful,' cried Ellie.
An alien saw them.

The alien abducted Ellie and Teddy and went into a UFO. They got captured.

Ellie and the alien made friends. He showed her the stars.

A huge monster saw the spaceship and licked it with his long tongue.

The alien and Spencer took Ellie home and she waved goodbye.

Daniel Toogood (6)
Lickey Hills Primary School, Rednal

Jed's Magical Adventure

One frosty night, Jess had a shadow on her wall. It was a magic elf.

Could the magic elf protect Jess against the mommy dragon?

The elf sure knew how to run.

Jess and the elf got on a unicorn and flew away.

The wicked witch cast a spell on the bear and killed it.

They flew away.

Jed Rowland (7)
Lickey Hills Primary School, Rednal

140

Shay's Magical Adventure

They went on a powerful unicorn.

They met an angry, fierce dragon.

They ran as fast as they could.

They met the unicorn again.

But then they met a wicked witch.

They flew home on a magic broomstick.

Shay Moroney (6)
Lickey Hills Primary School, Rednal

Isabelle's Magical Adventure

Ellie and Spencer arrived on a path and jumped on a beautiful unicorn.

Suddenly, they saw a massive, fierce dragon.
'Wow!' said Ellie.

'Run for your life!' said Spencer.

'Hip, hip, hooray! We are saved.'

Then they saw a witch who asked, 'Where are you going?'

They said, 'We are flying home on your broomstick.'

Isabelle Forrest-Anderson (6)
Lickey Hills Primary School, Rednal

Georgia's Space Story

They went higher and higher until they reached a beautiful planet. It was massive.

They landed on this planet. They were just collecting stars but an alien saw them.

The alien wanted a friend, so he sucked them into his spaceship. It was gooey inside.

Soon they were riding through the universe. It was a splendid view of the stars.

Suddenly, a horrible monster popped up. It nearly ate them, but they defeated it by shooting lasers at it.

Now it was time to go home.

Georgia Ralston (6)
Lickey Hills Primary School, Rednal

143

Mia's Jungle Tale

Once upon a time Ellie and Spencer the elf were swinging on vines.

Next, they went for a walk, then they were shocked.
'A snake!' Ellie shouted.

They met a horrible snake. It tried to eat them, but they ran away.

They met a friendly lion and the lion helped them.

The magical lion ran with Ellie, her teddy and Spencer the elf on his back.

In the moonlit darkness, they went back on the vines to go home to bed.

Mia Trivett (7)
Lickey Hills Primary School, Rednal

144

Matthew's Pirate Adventure

They went in a little boat because it was the only way to reach Coconut Island.

Spencer took Ellie to a treasure chest he had found buried in the golden sand.

Suddenly, a mean pirate appeared and stole the treasure.

The pirate took them to his massive ship and made them walk off the wooden plank.

Ellie was very scared, but Spencer's dolphin friends rescued them.

Spencer took Ellie home and Ellie said, 'What an adventure!'

Matthew Walker (6)
Lickey Hills Primary School, Rednal

Anna's Zoo Adventure

When they had landed, they were at the zoo.

They both had a ride on an elephant, even Teddy.

The elephant took them to visit the panda and her cubs.

They got back on the elephant and where did they go next?

They went to the monkeys and had a midnight feast.

The elephant took Ellie home and they all said goodbye.

Anna Parker (6)
Lickey Hills Primary School, Rednal

Nevaeh's Magical Adventure

Ellie went on a unicorn with an elf. When they got there, a witch said, 'Stop!'
'Why?' asked Ellie.
'Because you are not allowed.'

Ellie saw a dragon. He blew fire at Ellie and the elf.

The children ran away from the dragon.

The unicorn took the children back home.

Then at home there was a witch.

They rode a broom.

Nevaeh Anderson (6)
Lickey Hills Primary School, Rednal

Miriam's Magical Adventure

At the land it was called Magical Land. The first thing they did was go on a unicorn.

Second, they went on a dragon ride.
'It was scary,' said Ellie.

But it wasn't a ride, it was a real dragon! The dragon chased them.

They had another ride on the unicorn, but this time they had a long ride.

They found a witch in the lollipop house. She wanted to put them in the oven.

But they found her broom and they went home.

Miriam Robinson (5)
Lickey Hills Primary School, Rednal

148

Demi-Rose's Magical Adventure

At the land called Magical Land, the children went on a unicorn.

Next, they saw a dragon. They were scared as it was scary.

They ran away because it was scary.

They loved going on the unicorn.

They met a witch.

They went on the witch's broom.

Demi-Rose Williams (5)
Lickey Hills Primary School, Rednal

Nahum's Pirate Adventure

Spencer rowed the boat to an island.

They found treasure on the island. Spencer said, 'Look over there.'

'Oi you! What are you doing? Do not touch that. You boy, walk the plank.'

He walked the plank but the dolphins rescued him.
'You are next.'
Then another dolphin came.

The dolphins rode off.

They lived happily ever after.

Nahum John (5)
Lickey Hills Primary School, Rednal

Liberty's Magical Adventure

They arrived at a place and they saw a unicorn.

Then they came across a dragon. They were scared.

They ran away from the dragon.

They got on the unicorn. They rode on the unicorn.

Then they came across a witch. They were sad.

They went on the broomstick to their house.

Liberty Willis (6)
Lickey Hills Primary School, Rednal

Samuel's Pirate Adventure

They went to the beach and saw treasure.

They found the treasure but the pirates had it.

The pirate arrived. The pirate said 'It's our treasure.'

They jumped in the water. The dolphins took them home.

'It was fun,' they said.

A path took them home.

Samuel Lewis (5)
Lickey Hills Primary School, Rednal

Holly's Magical Adventure

They arrived at a magical place. They saw a unicorn.

Then they came across a dragon. They were scared.

They ran away from the dragon.

They got on the unicorn. They rode on the unicorn.

Then they came across a witch. They were sad.

They went on the broomstick to their house.

Holly Murphy (5)
Lickey Hills Primary School, Rednal

Amelia's Magical Adventure

Once there were some children. Their names were Jack and Serra.

Then they had an adventure. They saw a dragon!

They ran away from the fires from the dragon's face.

Then they rode a unicorn.
'This is fun,' said Jack.

After that they saw a witch, but the witch was kind.

Then they rode back home again on the witch's broom.

Amelia Geddes (6)
Lickey Hills Primary School, Rednal

154

Alice's Zoo Adventure

When they got there, there was an elephant.

The elephant went to see baby bear.

She saw a panda. She cuddled panda.

She kept walking until …

She saw a monkey. She was eating bananas.

Then she needed to go.

Alice McGlynn (5)
Lickey Hills Primary School, Rednal

Amalie's Magical Adventure

One magical night they saw a unicorn.
'Wow!' said Ellie and Spencer. They were surprised.

They saw some fire behind a tree. It was a dragon!
Ellie said, 'Run!'

Ellie said, 'Run faster, we need to get away!'
Teddy ran too. Teddy was sad, he was crying.

Ellie was safe now and Spencer was safe too. Ellie was crying her eyes out and she was cuddling Teddy.

They met a witch. It was a horrible witch. The witch made a spell on the children.

That made them fly way up high where the moon was and some clouds. Teddy nearly fell off.

Amalie Deegan (5)
Lickey Hills Primary School, Rednal

Frankie's Magical Adventure

Soon they arrived at magical land. They met a unicorn. It was a friendly unicorn, it was a magical unicorn.

Then they met a dragon. He was fierce. He didn't like anybody because he was fierce.

Then they had to run away because he was evil, he was really fierce.

Then they had to go home but the unicorn took them to the wrong place. They said, 'Oh no!'

The unicorn took them to a witch. The witch was evil. They didn't like the witch.

Then they flew home.

Frankie Johnson (5)
Lickey Hills Primary School, Rednal

Ellie's Space Story

At space there was an alien. The alien was in a flying saucer.

They saw an alien. It was a nice alien. The alien loved Ellie and Ellie loved the alien.

It brought Ellie and her teddy bear up and the stars were shining.

Ellie and the alien went round and round. The stars were shining bright.

There was a nasty alien. He was putting his tongue under the flying saucer.

'Goodbye,' said Ellie. 'Shall we go on another adventure next time?'

Ellie Griffiths (5)
Lickey Hills Primary School, Rednal

Moor Green
Primary School
Moseley

Daniel's Magical Adventure

One day Tom and Carol were on a gorgeous unicorn.

Tom and Carol were daydreaming when they fell down.

Soon they saw a dragon. They felt anxious.

But they found the unicorn and had a ride.

Tom and Carol found themselves with a witch. The witch gave the teddy a lollipop. Oh no, he was on the witch's team!

Never mind, they safely found their way home on a broomstick.

Daniel Hoxha (6)
Moor Green Primary School, Moseley

Diazan's Pirate Adventure

Once upon a time, one dark and dingy night, two kids woke up.

They found treasure, but then pirates came.

They wanted to have it.

Then they took them to their ship and threw them off.

Then they got on two dolphins and got back to shore.

They went home.

Diazan Yafai (6)
Moor Green Primary School, Moseley

161

Lesedi Jungle Tale

Once upon a time, Sophie and Joseph were swinging through the open vines. They had thorns on them.

Suddenly, snakes slithered from under the leaves. Joseph and Sophie were terrified.

So they ran away. When they went, it took a long, long time.

Finally, they came to a lion and they thought he was going to bite.

But he didn't. He gave them a ride.

They were safe from the snakes.

Lesedi Ncube (6)
Moor Green Primary School, Moseley

Bradley's Pirate Adventure

Two people were having a nice time rowing to the island.

Suddenly, they found the old, shiny treasure.

But just then, a pirate scared the people.

They made the boy walk the plank.

The dolphins took the boy and girl home.

They arrived home safely.

Bradley Davenport-Lynock (7)
Moor Green Primary School, Moseley

163

Oakfield Primary School
Rugby

Ashleigh's Magical Adventure

In magical world! First they met a unicorn and they flew into the air.

They met a fierce dragon with spikes. Spencer and Ellie ran away, but the dragon just followed.

So they ran away and hid. The dragon went away.
Ellie said, 'Phew!'

Next, they met the unicorn again and they flew in the air. They landed on a hill.

Then they bumped into a witch. Ellie said sorry. The witch was shocked, so she laughed.

Ellie screamed so Spencer got a key and they were free and they got the witch's broom and flew home.

Ashleigh Parker (7)
Oakfield Primary School, Rugby

Julia's Magical Adventure

Ellie rode on a unicorn quickly in the streets. The sun was rising.

Later on, a dragon came to see Ellie and Spencer.

After a while, the dragon was very cross at Ellie and Spencer.

Before long, Ellie and Spencer again got on the unicorn.

After that the witch came to Ellie and Spencer.

At the end, Ellie and Spencer went back home with a broomstick.

Julia Zak (6)
Oakfield Primary School, Rugby

Róisín's Pirate Adventure

Ellie and Spencer were rowing a boat. Soon they arrived.

They found some treasure and looked inside. They saw gold.

Next, Ellie and Spencer met a pirate.

They went with the pirate to his ship.

They played with the dolphins.

Soon it was time to go home.

Róisín Larkin (6)
Oakfield Primary School, Rugby

Elizabeth's Pirate Adventure

Ellie and Spencer found a boat and went on it.

They found some treasure on an island.

Suddenly, a pirate came with a sharp sword.

The pirate put Spencer on the plank. He was scared.

Some dolphins came to rescue Spencer and Ellie.

Then they were safe and sound at home.

Elizabeth Pipes (7)
Oakfield Primary School, Rugby

169

Sophie's Zoo Adventure

Ellie and Spencer arrived at the zoo.

Ellie rode on the elephant with the bear.

They rode to see the panda.

The panda was too big to get on the elephant.

Ellie and a gorilla had a banana. Bear and Spencer didn't want one.

'Bye Spencer and elephant.'
They went home for tea.

Sophie Marshall (6)
Oakfield Primary School, Rugby

Emily-Mae's Jungle Tale

In the jungle! Ellie and Spencer met a bear and swung on a rope with him.

Ellie and Spencer saw a snake. They knew it wasn't friendly.

Ellie and Spencer ran away.

They met a lion. They didn't know if it was friendly.

But it was so they rode on it.

They saw Ellie's home, so they got a vine and swung home.

Emily-Mae Lewis (6)
Oakfield Primary School, Rugby

Tyler's Space Story

They flew in space. It was really fun. Ellie was holding her teddy.

They landed on Mars. They were collecting stars.

An alien picked up Ellie and Spencer. It was a spaceship.

They waved to the other alien. Spencer was shouting.

A monster crunched its jaws. Ellie and Spencer were terrified.

Ellie said goodbye to Spencer and Spencer went.

Tyler Rea (6)
Oakfield Primary School, Rugby

Szymon's Pirate Adventure

At the sea, Ellie and Spencer fell into a boat and sailed to the island.

When they sailed to the island, they found a box. They opened the box and it was treasure.

Next, they had found a pirate with a brand new sword.

The pirate stole the treasure and ran off with it.

Then some big fish came and saved them.

They took Spencer and Ellie back home.

Szymon Jazewicz (7)
Oakfield Primary School, Rugby

Warren's Magical Adventure

… to a magical world. First they rode a unicorn across the path.

Suddenly, they met a blue dragon and it blew fire.

Spencer and Ellie ran away across the path.

Again, they hopped on the unicorn and it trotted away.

Then they met a bad witch. The bear loved the lollies.

They flew away on the witch's broomstick.

Warren Trezise (6)
Oakfield Primary School, Rugby

174

Ashton's Pirate Adventure

Ellie and Spencer were rowing in a boat.

'A treasure box!' said Spencer.

Then they saw a pirate.

Spencer had to walk the plank.

They were rescued by dolphins who took them for a ride.

They were safe and they walked home.

Ashton Kuka (6)
Oakfield Primary School, Rugby

Triston's Magical Adventure

Ellie and Spencer met a unicorn.

Then they met a green, angry, nasty dragon.

They all ran away from the dragon.

The unicorn saved them.

They met a bad witch.

They went home on her broomstick.

Triston Kuka (6)
Oakfield Primary School, Rugby

Aidan's Pirate Adventure

They went on a boat. Ellie hugged her teddy.

They came to an island and they saw treasure.

They saw a pirate.
'A pirate!' said Ellie.

The pirate made them walk the plank.

Instead, they went on dolphins.

The dolphins dropped Ellie and Spencer back home.

Aidan Saunders (6)
Oakfield Primary School, Rugby

Jack's Zoo Adventure

Spencer and Ellie had arrived at the zoo.

They had a ride on the elephant and the bear was on the elephant's trunk.

Soon Spencer and Ellie met a friendly panda.

Next, they took a ride on an elephant's back.

Then they met a gorilla eating a banana.

Spencer took Ellie home on the elephant.

Jack Sutcliffe (7)
Oakfield Primary School, Rugby

Riley's Zoo Adventure

Tulip and Sam went to the zoo.

The elephant gave them a lift.

Then they went to a panda.

Then they went to the monkey.

The monkey and Tulip had a banana.

Finally, it was time to go home.

Riley Perkins (5)
Oakfield Primary School, Rugby

Oakley's Zoo Adventure

Dan and Tamzin went on an elephant ride.

They went around the zoo.

The boy went to the panda.

They got on the elephant.

They met a monkey.

At the end they said goodbye.

Oakley Green (5)
Oakfield Primary School, Rugby

St Anthony's RC School
Kingshurst

Jessica's Jungle Tale

Jessica and Jack went to the jungle. They had fun swinging on the ropes with the monkeys.

They went for a walk and found a snake called Sid. He wasn't very friendly.

Jessica and Jack ran away from Sid as he hissed at them and made himself big and scary.

Round the corner they saw a friendly lion called Lenny. He asked if they wanted to meet his family.

They rode on his back and met his cubs, Lily and Lucy. They had fun.

Soon, it was time to go so they swung on the rope trees all the way home.

Jessica Woodward (7)
St Anthony's RC School, Kingshurst

Timberley Primary School
Shard End

Anam's Pirate Adventure

Once upon a time there was a girl and a boy. They went on a boat in the night.

When they arrived there, they found some treasure. When they opened the box they found some money.

When they were going to take some, a pirate came and he said, 'That's mine.'
'Sorry.'
'It's OK.'

They went on the pirate's ship. The boy was going to jump off the plank.

Then he jumped off it and they went on dolphins.

Then they went off and they found home.

Anam Lone (6)
Timberley Primary School, Shard End

Joshua's Pirate Adventure

Once upon a time there was a boy and a girl rowing in a boat.

Then they found treasure on the beach.

Then the little girl and boy saw a pirate.

The pirate said, 'Walk the plank.'

The little boy was scared.

Then the little boy found some dolphins, they went on them.

They walked back to their house and they had a cup of tea.

Joshua Smith (6)
Timberley Primary School, Shard End

185

Karis' Jungle Tale

Once upon a time two children and a teddy bear were swinging on vines.

Soon they saw a snake. The children were very scared.

Then they ran away as fast as they could.

Soon they saw a lion. The lion offered them a lift.

Then they climbed onto the lion.

Then they went home.

Karis Glass (7)

Timberley Primary School, Shard End

Zeruiah's Jungle Tale

They went swinging on the vines.

They met a snake.

They ran away.

They saw a lion.

They went on the lion.

They went home.

Zeruiah Thompson (5)
Timberley Primary School, Shard End

Robert's Jungle Tale

They swung through the trees.

They met a snake.

They ran away.

They met a lion.

They rode on the lion.

They went home on the vines.

Robert Wesley (6)
Timberley Primary School, Shard End

Harry's Space Story

An alien pulled two children into outer space and a teddy bear was asleep.

They were collecting some stars to take home and an alien saw them.

The alien pulled the little girl into the spaceship to show her around the moon.

The alien showed the little girl the different stars.

A big king alien came to say, 'Take the children back home.'

The alien said goodbye.

Harry Hughes (7)
Timberley Primary School, Shard End

189

Aisia-May's Zoo Adventure

Once upon a time a girl went to the zoo with a boy and teddy. They saw an elephant popping out the gate.

They went on a ride on an elephant and teddy was scared. He was clinging on.

Then they went to see a panda. The panda was squeezing the teddy. The panda had a baby.

They were heading home on the elephant. Teddy was still scared. The girl was happy.

When they were going home they saw a monkey with a banana.

Then she was at home. The boy was on the elephant and waved.

Aisia-May Waugh (6)
Timberley Primary School, Shard End

Chant'e's Jungle Tale

Chloe , Jack and Teddy were overjoyed because they were going to go on their journey.

Chloe, Jack and Teddy were halfway on their journey and a terrifying snake scared them.

The snake said, 'I'm going to eat you!'
Chloe, Jack and Teddy ran away.

Chloe, Jack and Teddy met a scary lion.

The lion wasn't really scary. He was a lovely lion and took them home.

Chloe, Jack and Teddy swung through the trees on their way home.

Chant'e Masih (6)
Timberley Primary School, Shard End

Sania's Magical Adventure

The girl and boy jumped on the unicorn, then they whooshed off through the air.

Then they met a scary dragon that blew out hot and orange fire. They were scared.

Then they ran away and the dragon followed them. Teddy ran with them.

They managed to escape from the dragon and the unicorn whooshed off again.

Then they met a nasty, ugly and horrible witch who had sharp nails on her fingers.

They managed to escape from the witch by going on her broom. Teddy was hanging off the back of the broom.

Sania Liaqat (6)
Timberley Primary School, Shard End

Azmat's Space Story

Once upon a time a girl and boy flew out of their home.

They got to an alien land. The alien saw them and laughed.

The alien got the girl and put her in his spaceship.

They flew up into space.

They were scared.

The girl went home and went back to sleep.

Azmat Mohammad (6)
Timberley Primary School, Shard End

Luqman's Jungle Tale

First they swung on the trees to see lots of animals.

Then they saw the snake. The snake had a long neck.

The snake scared them away. Then they ran away.

Then they met a lion. It was nice.

They had a ride on the lion.

Then they went back home.

Luqman Amin (6)
Timberley Primary School, Shard End

Lisa's Space Story

Once upon a time there were two children. There was a boy who had wings and a girl.

The children landed on the moon. An alien was spying on the children.

Then a spaceship came. The spaceship took the girl and her teddy.

The alien made friends. The girl was happy looking at the stars.

Suddenly, an eight-legged creature came. The creature had a long tongue. The creature had three eyes.

The alien took the girl home. She said, 'Thank you for the ride.'

Lisa Bird (7)
Timberley Primary School, Shard End

195

Jaward's Pirate Adventure

Once there were two children. They found a boat and they sailed away.

The children stopped at an island. On that island they found lots of gold.

But then a pirate saw them and he said, 'That's my gold!'

The pirate took them to his ship and he said, 'You have to walk the plank!'

But just then two dolphins saved them.

The dolphins took them back to dry land and they walked back home.

Jaward Manzoor (6)
Timberley Primary School, Shard End

Yusra's Jungle Tale

Once upon a time there was a girl and boy and their names were Sam and Adam. They were in a jungle.

We saw a snake. The snake wanted to eat Sam and Adam. The snake had a long tongue.

Sam and Adam ran away from the snake. They never saw the snake ever again.

Sam and Adam saw a lion. Sam and Adam were sad, the lion was happy.

Sam and Adam were happy too.

Yusra Mahamoud (6)
Timberley Primary School, Shard End

197

Eleni's Pirate Adventure

They went in a boat.

They found a treasure chest with money in it.

A pirate came to them. 'Get off my money,' he said.

They went on a boat. Spencer had to get off because he was being naughty.

Then Spencer said, 'Do you want to get a ride on the dolphin?'

'Do you want to go home?'
'Yes, I do,' she said.

Eleni Jayne Hewitt (5)
Timberley Primary School, Shard End

Fatima's Pirate Adventure

Tanya and Jack were rowing the boat to the island.

Tanya and Jack were hiding from the pirate when he pirate got home.

They were scared. Tanya and Jack ran away from the pirate.

Tanya and Jack were made to walk the plank.

Tanya and Jack had a ride on the dolphins.

'I love you,' said Jack.
'I love you too,' said Tanya.

Fatima Bibi (6)
Timberley Primary School, Shard End

Harrison's Pirate Adventure

One Sunday, the pirates came to the island.

They got off the boat and they got the treasure.

Then a pirate came and stole the treasure.

The pirate got the boy and fell into the water.

The dolphins helped them to get home.

'What an adventure! Now it's time for bed.'

Harrison Taylor (7)
Timberley Primary School, Shard End

Ward End Primary School
Ward End

Ibrahim's Zoo Adventure

One sunny day, Ben and Sally went to the zoo and Ben was really happy.

After that, Ben thought there was an earthquake, but then he looked the other way and saw an elephant.

Then Ben and Sally found a panda and Sally hugged one and Ben held a baby panda.

Next, they rode on the elephant.

After that they ate a banana with a monkey.

Finally, Sally and Ben went home on an elephant. They said goodbye.

Ibrahim Ajmal (6)
Ward End Primary School, Ward End

Kainat's Space Story

They were going to space, the girl, the boy and the girl's teddy.

They landed on a planet and the boy had stars in his hand.

Then a spaceship got the girl and the teddy and the girl was scared.

Then there were two spaceships and the girl wasn't scared anymore, she was having fun.

After that they saw a monster on a planet and they were all scared.

Finally, the boy and the alien took the girl and the teddy home.

Kainat Raja (7)
Ward End Primary School, Ward End

Imarah's Pirate Adventure

Ellie spotted a small island far away. So Spencer sailed the boat to the island.

They got off the boat onto the island. There they saw a treasure chest.

They opened the treasure chest. They heard a voice from behind: 'Ahoy!'
They looked, it was a scary pirate.

Spencer ran away from the horrid pirate. Ellie followed him.

They both jumped onto the dolphins' backs. The dolphins rescued them from the pirate.

At last they were home. The adventure was over.

Imarah Shahzad (6)
Ward End Primary School, Ward End

Michaela's Jungle Tale

They are swinging from tree to tree.

They see a snake and are scared.

They are running away from the snake.

They see a tiger and are a bit frightened.

They get on the tiger and they ride on it.

They get home swinging from tree to tree.

Michaela Sheppard (6)
Ward End Primary School, Ward End

Mustafa's Jungle Tale

They arrived at a wonderful, huge jungle full of wild animals.

Soon they met a very bad snake sticking his tongue out.

The snake hissed and scared them away.

Meanwhile, they met a very polite lion named Sam.

The lion took the two for a little walk.

At the end of the adventure, Peter took Molly home.

Mustafa Mohammad Ishaq Mohiuddin (6)
Ward End Primary School, Ward End

Laila's Space Story

In a cold and dark place with beautiful stars.

Spencer thought he would collect stars for Ellie but someone was watching.

It was Roofus. 'Would you like to see my world?'

They were waving to other aliens and were on their way home when …

There was a monster with a big tongue and three eyes.

He wanted his stars back. Ellie, Roofus and Spencer threw them into the sky so they could get Ellie home. At home in bed, Ellie whispered, 'I wonder what tomorrow's adventure will be?'

Laila Hussain (6)
Ward End Primary School, Ward End

Sidra's Pirate Adventure

Ellie and Spencer were flying over the sea. They saw a boat. Spencer rowed the boat to the island.

Ellie and Spencer went on the land and found a box of treasure.

A mean pirate said, 'Why are you messing with my treasure?' He took his sword out and played with it.

The mean pirate tried to kill Ellie and Spencer by pushing them into the sea.

Then two dolphins saved Ellie and Spencer and took them to the land.

Ellie and Spencer were happy. They had fun and went back home.

Sidra Ali (6)
Ward End Primary School, Ward End

Mohammed Eesah's Jungle Tale

They swung on a vine.

They saw a snake.

They ran away from the snake.

On the way they saw a lion.

The lion gave them a ride.

They went home.

Mohammed Eesah Khan (6)
Ward End Primary School, Ward End

Lauren's Jungle Tale

Ellie, Spencer and Ted were happy because they were swinging and they were excited at the adventure to come.

When they stopped, they saw a snake and they were scared of the snake biting them.

When the snake stuck out his tongue, Ellie, Spencer and ted ran away because they thought the snake was going to bite them.

As they walked, they heard a roar and they saw something move in the bushes. It was a lion. They were shocked. They thought it was something else.

They got on the lion's back. Spencer put a magic spell on the lion. 'Go, and run to Ellie's house before it is morning.'

Ellie got off the lion's back and swung to the house.

Lauren Groves (6)
Ward End Primary School, Ward End

210

Woodloes Primary School
Warwick

Evie's Magical Adventure

Soon they were in a magical land far, far away. A unicorn came and flew them over the candy fields.

A fierce dragon blew fire at them, but Ellie always had a plan.

'Run!' They ran for their lives.

In the nick of time, the unicorn came and rescued them.

An evil witch said, 'Try one of my power lollies.'
But they didn't, she couldn't be trusted.

They flew back on a broomstick. *Was it a dream,* thought Ellie.

Evie Cooke (7)
Woodloes Primary School, Warwick

Ella's Jungle Tale

They swung on a vine in the jungle and they swung through the trees. 'Watch out!' said Ellie. There was a bush.

They met a snake. It looked friendly but it wasn't as they found out. Spencer put his hand over his mouth. Ellie said, 'Don't you taste it.'

'Run!' said Ellie. They all ran except Ellie's teddy. Then the teddy soon realised that they had run, so he ran too.

They met a lion. This time, Ellie put her hand on her mouth. It looked mean.

But it wasn't, it was playful and cuddly. They got on the lion and ran through the jungle.

Then after the adventure, they swung home on the vines.

Ella Johnson (6)
Woodloes Primary School, Warwick

Isaac's Jungle Tale

Soon they came to a jungle! Ellie was smiling an enormous smile as she swung through the trees.

Then Spencer and Ellie saw a snake! The snake was fierce. Ellie looked at the snake.

Ellie and Spencer had to run so they did and they said, 'Run! Run for your life!'

Then they met a lion. 'Mmm, you're a big lion!' said Ellie. Spencer just looked at the lion.

Then Ellie and Spencer had a ride on the lion. Ellie said, 'This is fun.' Spencer said, 'I agree.'

After that, Ellie and Spencer headed back home on the swinging trees.

Isaac Tipson (6)
Woodloes Primary School, Warwick

Chloe's Space Story

Soon they arrived in space.

When they were on the moon, they met an alien. 'Run!'

Then Ellie and her teddy got lifted up into the alien ship.

They zoomed down to the universe.

They went over another planet. There was another alien. It stuck its tongue out and pushed the ship and made it go faster.

Ellie got dropped on her pathway.

Chloe Whittle (6)
Woodloes Primary School, Warwick

Celyn's Space Story

They arrived in space. They were flying.

They sat on the moon. In the distance there was an alien.

Then its spaceship sucked Ellie and her teddy. They were in it!

'Eek!' Ellie shrieked.
'Don't be scared. Do you want to go flying?'
'Yes!'
So they did.

Ellie and the alien saw a monster. They flew away.

Then they dropped her off at her house.

Celyn Sanders (6)
Woodloes Primary School, Warwick

Zarak's Pirate Adventure

Ellie and Spencer rowed a boat. Soon, they arrived at an island. It was very hot there.

Ellie found a treasure chest full of gold and crowns. Spencer shouted, 'Pirates in the sea!'

'Arrr! Give me back my treasure, children!' shouted Captain Hook.

'You'll be dropped in the sea, elf.'
Boing, boing, boing! Was the sound of the plank.

The blue dolphins saved Ellie and Spencer. 'We will be back home soon, Ellie cried.

'We are home already,' Spencer shouted. 'Come to my house.'

Zarak Rahman (6)
Woodloes Primary School, Warwick

Paris' Zoo Adventure

Once upon a time there was a nice girl called and Ellie and a boy called Spencer.

When they arrived at the elephants, Ellie and Spencer climbed up onto them.

They came to black and white animals.
'What is that?' cried Ellie.
'It's a panda being nice.'

'The grey elephant gave us a good ride,' smiled Ellie.

Ellie met a monkey. 'Hello, would you like a snack?'
'Yes, I love snacks.'

'It's time to come home,' shouted Mum.
'OK, Mum.'

Paris Chanel-Smith (6)
Woodloes Primary School, Warwick

Matthew's Jungle Tale

They found themselves swinging on branches from a tree. They were having fun. 'Wahoo!' they said.

But then a strong snake came and he was ready to pounce on Ellie and the scared elf.

They both went. 'Run!' panted Spencer. 'If we run a bit faster, we could get to a hiding place.'

'Phew, that was close.' Out of the corner of Ellie's eye she saw a lion.

She asked, 'Can we have a ride?'
'Yes, to the left,' said Spencer. 'Back to Ellie's house.'

When they got back, they were relieved. They were having fun swinging on branches.

Matthew Robinson (7)
Woodloes Primary School, Warwick

Thomas' Magical Adventure

In a magical land of unicorns and dragons …

Spencer and Ellie saw a dragon. It was very mean!

They ran away, a long way and said, 'Help! Help!'

They went on a pony. It was fun, very fun.

They saw an evil witch. She was horrid, she was ugly.

They flew back into Ellie's house and Ellie fell fast asleep.

Thomas Burdon (7)
Woodloes Primary School, Warwick

Wyken Croft
Primary School
Coventry

Edgar's Pirate Adventure

They arrived in a small boat and they saw an island. They started to paddle towards it.

When they got there, they found some treasure. Just then, Spencer saw a pirate ship.

'Ah!' they said as the captain walked out the ship. The captain captured the two of them.

They were in the ship. They started to walk the plank.

Just then two dolphins swam towards them. Just then they jumped on.

The dolphins took them home.

Edgar Roberts-Dalton (7)
Wyken Croft Primary School, Coventry

Gabrielle's Zoo Adventure

They arrived at a zoo. They ran inside the zoo to see the animals.

Spencer and Ellie had a ride on an elephant. They had fun on the big elephant.

Ellie and Spencer went to see a soft, furry panda. The panda had a cute baby panda.

They got on an elephant and Spencer saw another animal. It was a big monkey.

The big monkey gave Ellie a tasty banana.

Then it was time for the elf to go home.
'Goodbye,' said Ellie.
'Goodbye,' said Spencer.

Gabrielle Parkhill (6)
Wyken Croft Primary School, Coventry

Ria's Magical Adventure

At a magical land where a unicorn gave them a ride.

They stopped and there was a dragon.
'Can we get out?' Ellie asked.

'Run!' they both said together. Soon they got out of sight from the dragon.

The unicorn gave them a ride back again but …

They went past a witch. She had lollipops in her house.

The unicorn didn't come back but they found a giant paintbrush.

Ria Jassal (6)
Wyken Croft Primary School, Coventry

Nathan's Space Story

Soon they were out of space. There were sparkly stars.
'Wow!' said Ellie.

They landed on the moon. An alien was behind Ellie and Spencer. They picked stars.

Then a weird alien came in a spaceship. Ellie was pulled into the spaceship.

Ellie saw some other aliens coming for her.
'Bye,' said the alien.
She hopped in the spaceship.

Suddenly, a huge monster came. 'Argh!' shouted Ellie. The monster tried to get the spaceship.

Nathan Docherty (7)
Wyken Croft Primary School, Coventry

Derry's Zoo Adventure

Soon they had arrived at the zoo. They saw a big elephant. It was very nice.

The elephant said, 'Hop on.'
Ellie said, 'I see bamboo, look!'

The elf said, 'Look again.'
There was a huge panda.

They got back on the enormous elephant.

On the way they stopped and saw a monkey and got a banana.

Soon it was time to go.
'Goodbye,' said the elf.
'Bye,' said Ellie, 'sleep tight.'

Derry O'Neill (6)
Wyken Croft Primary School, Coventry

Casey's Zoo Adventure

At an African zoo.
'What a beautiful zoo,' said Ellie.
'Thanks,' said Spencer.

'I love that elephant,' said Spencer.
They climbed on.

'Arr!' said Spencer. 'I love this baby panda.'
'I like it too,' said Ellie.

Then they went back on the elephant.
'Whee!' they said.

They swung in the tree and ate a banana. They had really good time.

'Now we need to go home,' said Spencer.
'Bye,' said Ellie.
'Bye,' said Spencer.

Casey Branch (7)
Wyken Croft Primary School, Coventry

Erin's Zoo Adventure

Soon they had arrived at a loud zoo. Then they saw a big elephant.

Next, the elephant had some bamboo! After that Ellie was really happy.

Meanwhile, they saw a huge panda and he was very cute.

Then they went through the bushes and went very fast.

Later on they saw lots of monkeys, but they were eating lots of bananas.

But it was time to go.
'Bye,' Ellie said to Spencer.

Erin Johnson (6)
Wyken Croft Primary School, Coventry

Maariya's Magical Adventure

At a magical land. The elf took Ellie to a colourful, magical unicorn.

They rode on the unicorn.
'Argh!' screamed Ellie. It was a fierce, mean dragon.

They ran and ran. Meanwhile, a little teddy bear was running after them.

Soon they found a teddy bear. Ellie picked up the teddy bear and off they went.

Next, they found a wicked witch. The witch offered the teddy a lolly.
'No!' shouted Spencer.

Then the witch said, 'Have a ride on my broom.'
'Yes,' said Ellie and *zoom!* They arrived back home.

Maariya Imaan (6)
Wyken Croft Primary School, Coventry

229

The
End!

Young Writers Information

We hope you have enjoyed reading this book - and that you will continue to enjoy it in the coming years.

If you like reading and creative writing drop us a line, or give us a call, and we'll send you a free information pack.

Alternatively if you would like to order further copies of this book or any of our other titles, then please give us a call

or log onto our website at **www.youngwriters.co.uk**

Young Writers Information
Remus House
Coltsfoot Drive
Peterborough
PE2 9BF
(01733) 890066